How to Hide a Lion

Helen Stephens

ALISON GREEN BOOKS

One hot day,
a lion strolled
into a market square
to buy a hat.

But the townspeople were scared of lions,

so he ran away.

He ran as fast and as far as he could . . .

. . . and hid in a house in a garden. It was a play house,
and it belonged to a small girl called Iris.
"You can't hide there," said Iris, who wasn't scared of lions.
"That house is too small for you."

They went inside, so Iris could hide the lion properly. They had to be quiet, as mums and dads can be funny about having a lion in the house.

The lion let Iris pull the leaves out of his mane . . .

. . . and he showed her his paw where he had stepped on something sharp. "I'll put a plaster on that," said Iris.

It wasn't easy hiding a lion.

He was just too big . . .

too fluffy . . .

and too heavy, especially
when he was asleep.
And lions sleep a lot.

But when no one was looking,
the lion could come out to play.

They just had to be careful
not to be too noisy.

One evening, Iris's dad said, "They still haven't found that lion."
"I bet he's a kind lion," said Iris, from behind the sofa.
"There's no such thing as a kind lion," said her mum. "All lions will eat you."

The lion was worried,
but Iris comforted him.

Then she read him his favourite story. It was about a tiger who came to tea. He fell asleep halfway through, because lions sleep a lot.

And that was how everything went wrong.

Iris heard her mum coming up the stairs,

but it's hard to wake
a sleeping lion.

However, most lions will wake up
if a mum screams at them.

The lion raced out of the house . . .

. . . and found a hiding place where he could
still see Iris whenever she came into town.

Nobody noticed him.

Not the townspeople. Not even Iris.

And certainly not the two burglars, who broke into the Town Hall
and stole every single one of the Lord Mayor's candlesticks.

But the lion noticed them.

With a huge

ROAR!

he leapt off his pedestal . . .

... and stood on both the burglars
till the police came.

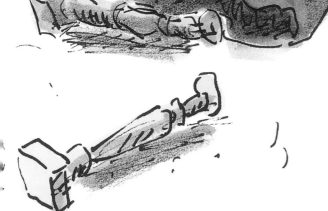

All the townspeople were amazed — except for Iris, who said, "I told you he was a kind lion."

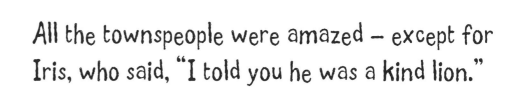

And that surprised everyone.

Now the lion was a hero. He didn't have to hide any more.
The townspeople held a special parade for him.
The Mayor said he could have anything he wanted.

The lion thought for a moment.
Then he asked for . . .

... a hat!

Which was all he'd come to town for in the first place.